Preface

David Antony Herbert originally began writing The 9th Pleasure creativity in the 9th month of 2007 based on personal relationships between the sea and nature.

As the short story unraveled layer upon layer, it became a delicate matter of holding precious gems of bearing within entangling formations of endless surrounding 9s.

The 9th Pleasure originated as an autobiography mixed in with the love of cultures after finding a unique string of pearls while writing about the perspective pleasures of defying time.

The parting side of the journey is an abstract poetry crossing set out to ask the universe questions about humanity, destiny, and weird worldly existence.

The 9th Pleasure

Lost Luster Of Pearls

by David Anthony Herbert

This book is dedicated to all those who seek truth
to the 9th pleasure.

Untold Journeys

These are some deep sea engravings from personal experiences with creative fire of exotic luster. A day may come when the deepest treasures come undone, but this is my cast away story.

After growing up in a unique family with a string of pearl brothers and sister, we quickly learned the value of interactions. We were fortunate to live in a colony deep underground near the underwater villages of a town called Saint Lu Lust.

Our community was surrounded by orchids of pods where we hunted and went looking for the deepest of trouble. It was fortunate for us to seek out under-layer dugouts where we snuck out every other tiding for exploring into the great unknown.

My family got along fairly well and we casually became the greatest of enemies from time to time. Living was both fun and tough growing up among the sea. Back in the deep crusting days, we did everything we could to rebel against power and any so called sea gathering.

As young gems, we played on aqua-grounds learning to flip and turn every which way in any surrounding vineyard. Breaking free upon foreign waters was forbidden, but so much fun of lust.

Finding the brisk streams of chaos became hangout spots among the guru of pearls. Taking challenges to see how deep a pearl can twirl in a sea vent twisted into some deadly battles of mind and soul.

Any family talks of lucid pleasure were kept on a secret fossil basis between cultured pearls. Digging too deep in the dark depths of decay appeared to be morbid and out of touch.

While approaching the crustacean age, all sea hell broke loose without boundaries. We conquered volcanoes, caused earthquakes, and plunged onto the shooting stars.

Finding pursuits of passionate pleasure mixed in with wild adventures turned into the ultimate treasure.

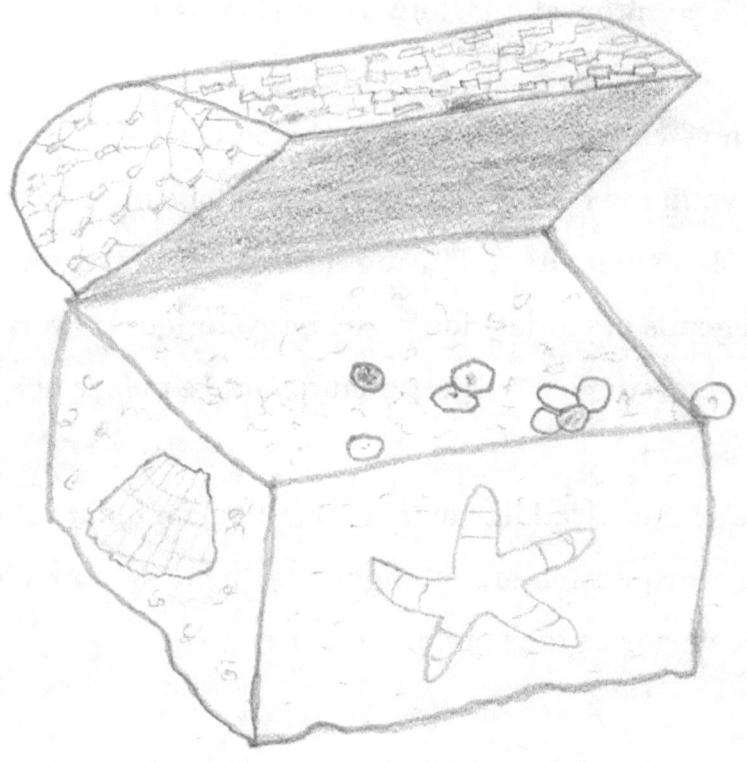

Great mysterious journeys of solitude slid beyond the realm of meaningful past history.

The arising family of pearls built shelters deep in the distant grounds. Lonely trails of deception sought out the weak and pure of heart at the hardest of times.

A secret truth formed out of the boundaries of a forbidden world. Stories among fortune and fantasy echoed into waking storms of distant reality.

A mysterious tribe known as the Stoney Roaks set out beyond the realms of ocean rises. No pearl has ever come back lusting after following these magical creatures. Legends of stories riddled with mysterious powers fell to the creasing ice glaciers melting above the ice age.

Time unraveled like an opening crack of lunar eclipse. The suspension of nothingness came to an abundant means for legions of floral life.

A growing intoxication of transformation set apart unity of some other worldly forces. An existence came from beyond reaching out a separation of matter and energy.

Traveling to the domains of different dimension became an imminent jolt of transformation. An era of lost consciousness made new grounds of becoming a genuine gem of timely fate.

A new found scenery of outer adaptation made youthful days a hypnotizing plunder of ignorance. A secret fortress of vanity was discovered while passing through the valley of divine spirits. Some awkward communication bared a naked truth of foreign entities with awareness.

A brilliant Stoney Roak appeared to display an oasis of polarizing pleasure. There was no more need to find any lair of misconception. Swift movements brought forth puzzling pieces of a mythical island at bay.

Adaptation became astounding to the tidal forces of mounting meadows. Instincts of bitter flavor dripped to the essence of soulful perception. Lost emotion drifted away from the sea floor bottom and flourished with wildlife as a thorny flower of blooming truth.

Relationships stemmed from the passionate growth of branching varieties. A colossal of dreams forged passion for the amending kin. This decadent quest of nobility made leaving an old world a life long journey of intertwined fate.

An Ancient Pearl Life Washed Ashore

In far distant years, the chance of falling in love came washing ashore. Life painted all these new meanings in unthinkable ways. Everlasting fate was colliding like stars in a bonding nebula. Time, matter, and energy melted away into a blissful drift. Beauty transformed into wondrous gifts of thought and feelings. Eternal tranquility opened up like a sea of red roses with heavenly scents shift shaping life.

A new fear of emptiness had surrounded me when this wandering happiness hit a deep black hole of extinction. Life cascaded with great uncertainty as much as the dark shaded over the night.

Shattered illusions began forming into endless caves of mercy without regret. There was a still silence while darkness crept into my own passionate fire of trust, faith, and light.

A mirage of past nightmares transformed pleasures with shadows of inner doubt. A real life horror story emerged at once without sorrow. Times of insanity paralyzed me with the poison of a stingray, yet strengthened me with an eye of the rising sea.

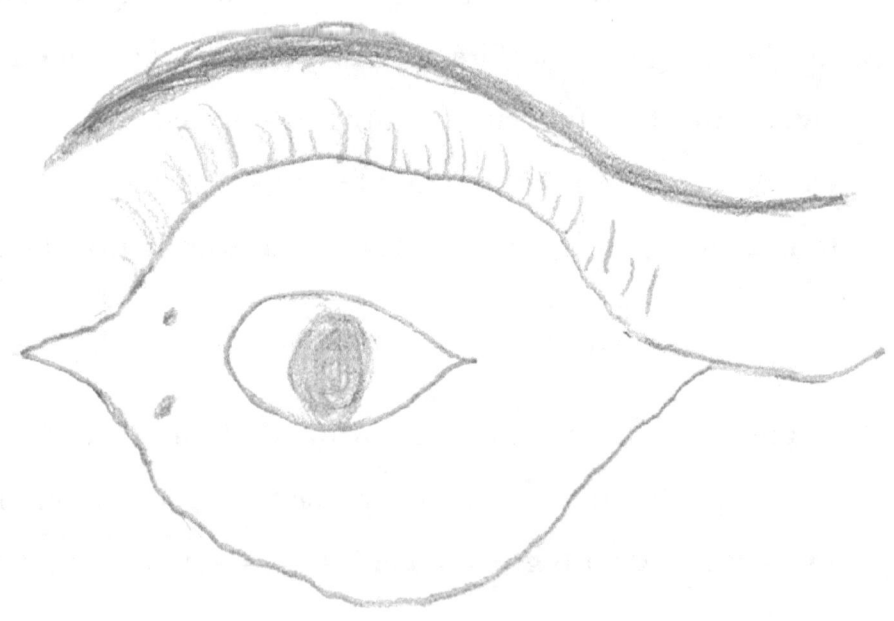

Moving on through this painful pleasure of life was as successfully failing as one could divinely believe. As days passed on, the inner roots began forming into new layers of deepening crust. These developing stages reformed creativity in unique places. Adapting in this exotic ground endured an aging process longer than grapes grow on wild vines among the stars.

One by one, affectionate relationships aged into withering seashells of the ancient past, while real life continued sprouting up with gatherings of seaweed and starfish. Swarming skies turned into shades of mystical colors with a passion of nurturing love. Nothing on the outside was made to luster or shine on the inside anymore.

Untangling this pearl inside an oyster within the great abyss made liberation a fossilized truth. Any hopeful chimes of harmonic bliss became a message in a bottle through a dividing ocean of heartfelt emotion. A whisper of songs tingles my outside layer as the undertow of tides collided beneath me time after time.

A legend of nine finite pearls withered unique inscriptions with gifts of pleasure including love, compassion, trust, peace, happiness, freedom, mindfulness, sacrifice, and 9.

Some of the most sacred and inner thoughts were unraveled each moment as they plunged up splashing the shores against the essence of life. My inner self exploded against the quivering horizons of beauty. Clusters of crabs scavenging nearby picked up pieces of honesty scattered throughout the sands of destiny.

The edge of reality morphed into fantasy while fading into a distant paradise of birds chirping melodies, puffy clouds shaping into doves, and flowers of magic pollinating my thoughts. A century of epics turned passionately through a diamond crystal of daydreams and reflections.

Gazing starfish washed up on endless shores from the raging storms with the king crab of exotic peace. Within a thunderous flash, a heart-shaped oyster opened up a dimension and swept me away to mesmerizing caverns of romance.

A passing vibrant tavern of twinkling jewels impressed notion of a shooting star waiting for a final destination. Jolting splashes of rainbow clouds lashed out beyond an invisible realm of misty skies.

Wandering stones sifted into images and writings. Drops of sediment fell about shaping a foundation of engraving clay-mations. Midnight became mysterious horizons while night no longer divided any days.

Dawn spread out prisms of rays transcending to the wilderness of an eternal flame. Echoes of nature merged together with a flora of sea life shape-shifting creatures. Strange tides lost my most creative seashell in a time of danger intoxicating me with a fear of loneliness.

Finding the quest back to the fire of tranquility submerged me further back to a rift of an underground veracity. The deepest ice ages formed over my shield cracking the inner strength of my parting pearl life. The passing of time twisted me in with the mural of a raging sea of desire.

Wars of fury broke icicles apart in the underground melting layers of caves. Mystifying sounds of musical history wandered into the precious hearts of bubbles popping from intensive pressure. An electrical cosmos of beauty passed over me with conductive integrity. The innocent seashells of protection divided from the clashing barrage of tidal dangers.

A revelation endured as pleasures neutralized in directions of opposing forces shaking my inner core to enlightenment.

Glowing vessels of seaweed drew near after disappearing in a faint idea of world conquest threatening all sides. Rivalries of sponges squashed together creating a mountain of underwater subways. Allies formed canyons of rock and cliffs finding any strays of flourishing life.

Opposing societies of wild weeds budded up with surrounding sea life trapping any jewels floating by. Moonlight jellyfish provided safe passage over the cliffs beneath the herds of seahorses. Enriched sea life gathered together to protect the sea from any space invaders.

Earthquakes ripped open the sea floors letting lava ooze to the wild. Splashing riptides forged through the valleys of land splitting way for the grandest of all canyons. A dying love of earthly lust settled into the exclamations of life.

Aquatic algae grew beside the rocky roads of bewildered enemies. After reaching to the shadowy shores of uncertainty, twirling butterflies touched my shell with delightful kisses. At last, the innocent imprints of origin sprang off to the distant horizons. A passionate wind blew past the covered grounds of lucky clovers with some reflective pleasures. Crawling critters kept creeping to the richest soils of the tropical underworlds.

Wicked warping coral thriving from a great barrier reef divided a worldly time continuum. The illusion of matter sparkled upon an ancient history of amber.

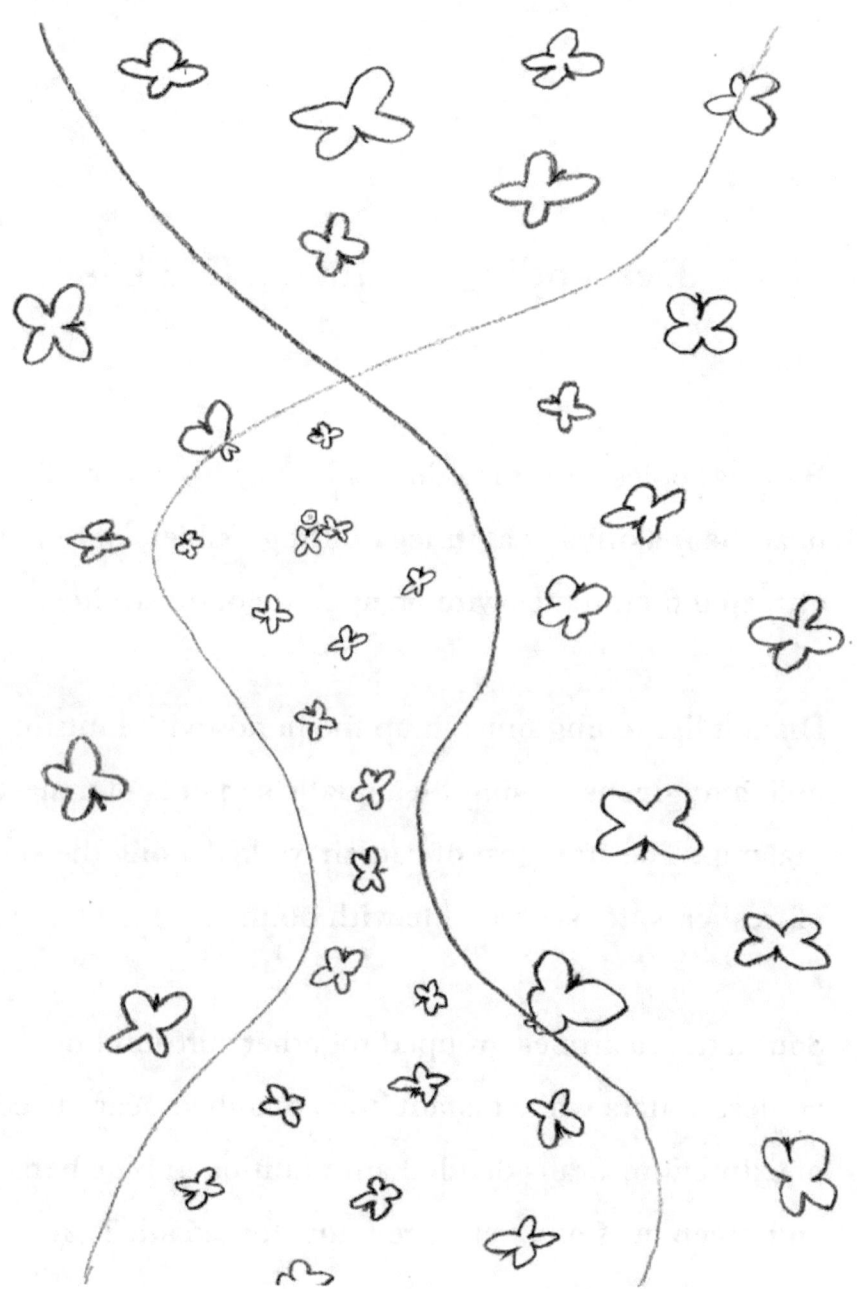

Descending Peninsula Of Love

Baby tadpoles squirmed downstream with kissing lips
near the makings of a prince bullfrog. Riblets of romance
attracted their mates with an appetite of mosquitoes.

Distant lightening bugs lit up the ponds with hints of
gold and greens teasing the aquatic serpents of majestic
makeup. The strangest of catfish walked along the shores
of fresher water seeking life with bounty.

Southern sea armies grouped together surrounding
endless waters while distant bugs marched near the edge
of extinction. Crabs divided ammunition of blue berries
and green peas and fishy predators forged shells of
defense for another outlandish enemy.

Straying on land, tribes of praying mantis tore up giant trees and leaves for protection from approaching armies gathering amongst the borders of the uncertainty. Rocks fell to the unjust cause of typhoons beside the breaking battlegrounds on the equator of immoral honesty.

Colossal knots of seaweed built up bridges of unique diversity. Leaders helped carry out orders with strict supremacy throughout all country. Hidden sea monkeys squandered up to the deadly paths of jewelry.

Then abruptly, some ice breaking storms neutralized conflict of opposing sides while skyscraping cliffs tumbled down onto the ocean floors of smoldering belief. Rising sea levels drowned islands of serenity sponging away the wild reigns of odyssey.

Flooding territories sank beneath the digesting sea of agony. Foes among friends unleashed their powers of berries onto the blue waters of battle tunes. A return fire of heaping relics cast onto the age of escaping beauty onto the ocean.

The mess of war was unleashed at once with the never ending rage of chaos. Sponges alongside cactus fought with the needless strength of progression. Unjust cause advanced into shadows of merciless aggression. The fear of isolation swarmed with disbelief near the souls of all emotion.

Flocks of seagulls saved each other with the swaying winds of western breezes. Frogs drifted their way on jellyfish springing away with their harvesting lilies. The wise owls swooped up the young as prowling vultures lingered about the bloodlines of the weeping.

Underwater islands ripened into aqua playgrounds for schools of fish and sunken ghost ships. Baby sharks grew appetites with razor teeth chomping up bait in any pathway of desire. Colored pearls hid amongst sea urchins and the sunken gold mines of a lost pearl dynasty.

Lion fish protected the cast away with left over treasure from the disappearing battle.

Rhubarb evoked a delightful taste for turtles with all the new found harbors. Murky waters washed the tides by shimmering pods of whales splashing through the daylight. Dolphins jumped behind echoing hymns of synchronous songs while sounds warping through time calling speeds of altering grace.

Wandering designs of life roam freely between the washed up shores of distinctive reality. Nine years of uncertainty passed by as sandy beaches plagued the wake of dying watery lands. The settlements of sand drew near while the dark storms of night flashed into fear.

Tiny winged creatures with Stoney Roak eyes saved many armies buried within time. Continuing rescue missions for eons to come evolved into epics for all chameleons.

An aquatic legion of misfits became heroes subsiding amongst the bleached coastlines of chaos. The sorrowful songs of mischief followed a world reign of tropical creators.

Species of dragon-flies whizzed to the flavor of dying seaweed and overcast beaches. The strength of surviving warriors brought forth an ever-lasting piece of vengeance.

A corridor without ends ignited a diamond dividing up pearls with an age of innocence. Endless allusions of love and harmony fused in with a shimmering fabled history.

The art of a beautiful unity illustrated a living fate of liberty. Forgiveness and acceptance vowed to a living legend of seeking prayers. Sincerity yielded a spirit of fire to scorch the fields of reclamation. Ancient tombstones with markings washed away with encryptions foretelling their fortune.

Dreams of the innocent healed the broken rainbows of a forbidding past. Purple and green gemstones radiated energy with untouchable luxury. Mountainous waterfalls trickled down the colorful cliffs of rocks chipping off the edges of stardom.

Tidal splashes of sea lava faded away from the purity of precious stones. The quivering fins of sea life vibrated to the coloring cores of their characteristics.

Mossy plants moisturized the ancient soils of awakened Bodhi trees. Bodacious chemistry instilled grazing land with devouring carnivores alongside with leafy green herbivores. Praying mantis returned to their home of poisonous mushrooms residing on the residue of dewy climate.

Whispers of a tropical village on cloud nine foretold an ancient dynasty of heritage. Tree veins nourished the lifelines of fruits, veggies, and flowers. Sapping tree scents sweetened the oxygen of early dew mornings.

Far away castles with frosty rooftops gleam the stone roads of hazy legends. A will of revelations emerged out to an independence of energy, spirit, and mystery. The fate of pleasure withered away with desire for all pearlings waiting to transpire.

Out from the innocence of time came forth the virtues of promising every day a new beginning with tidal endings to a trail of earthly makings...

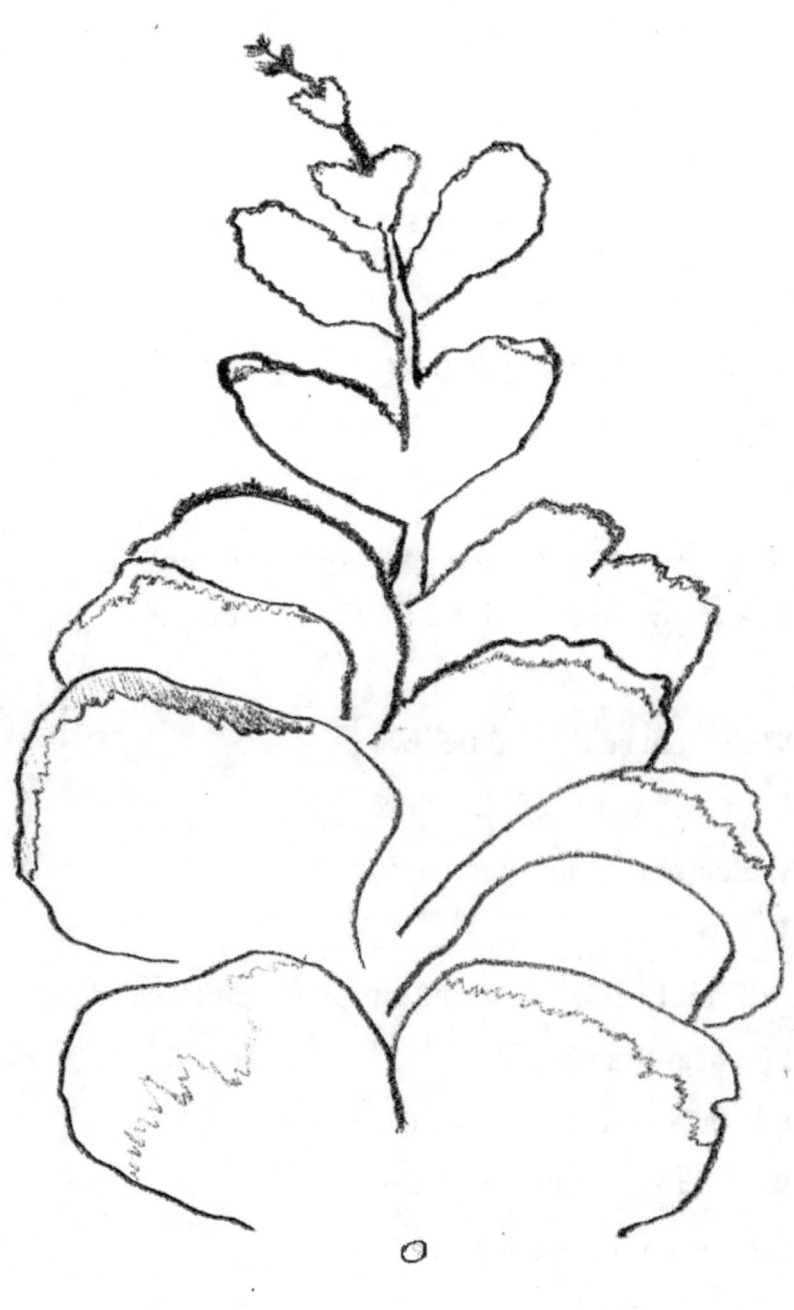

25

Abstract Poetry

What kind of pearly legends are surfacing?
Are you caught up in a perilous deception?

Would you follow a peaceful oblivious ending?
Would you jump in for a tragic beginning?

Which cause do you believe in?
Is there a belief of all reflecting?
Which one is not recollecting?

Are you becoming something you can't flee?
How can that be?
Or was it a leaf by some tree?
Which tree would you be?
Where would you meet?
Who will you be?

Have you become what you eat?

How much junk should you keep?

Can we talk about what you can't preach?

What is the deal?

What is for real?

Are you the real deal?

Or is this how you appeal?

How can you be so sure it's pure?

Is that all of what you believe?

Aren't words about what you perceive?

Maybe there is much doubt?

Maybe you're on the ninth cloud?

How high can you fly?

How old are you and how do you apply?

Will you read and write for one more try?

Who made us so darn shy?

Is there really a reason why?

Why are there so many shadows without a doubt?
Aren't there sunrises that do revolve?

Who can explain a shrinking theory making the biggest bang?
Would you roll the dice for a different tang?
Do nine million lives celebrate the same birthday each day?
Did someone set the world as a human stage?
Weren't you made with the same alien DNA?

Aren't numbers ruled with dice?
What are the odds of being the even slice?

Aren't we the oddly evens of the dividend of heaven?
How many shapes and sizes finally roll into seven?

How much salt spreads in the ocean or sea?
Are there as many bees on trees with so much honey?

Are you man enough to be male?
Do you care enough to be beautifully female?

Will there be a day when we remember everything?

Is there an original sin that gets you in?

What favorite color desires your skin?

Aren't you the leading icon?

Are you just a fib of fabrication?

Why do we forget so many dang things?

Is your fate threading on a needle of biology?

Can you start a deeper philosophy?

Have you been shown what's never been known?

What if no one knows how it goes?

Can you copy and paste yourself into a snow globe?

Would you recognize your own life better than your best friend?

Will you make the best illusion following this final conclusion?

Does night ever tuck in the scary day away?

Who figured out what makes time fly by?

What causes so many shades of grey?

Is life about connecting your fate?

Is there an escape that keeps you safe?

Is the root of all evil transforming good after all?

Is it illogical to ask the planet not to spin in the fall?

Are quantum light years explained without a timely tick?

Why didn't man jump over the moon instead of landing
on it?

Are new found planets found by man or out of the
ordinary?

Aren't new lines of code being created for digital
markings?

Do words just materialize in an artificial intelligent
dictionary?

Can the universe create the biggest black hole from junk
that doesn't matter?

Is the universe scented with an antique powder?

Would you like a 76 year ride on Halley's Comet?

Do universal symphonies compose their own grand cosmic opera?

Will future honeymooners fly to the moon for the cinema?

Is there any other comet that has the hots for the sun?

Wouldn't you travel in space with an ocean sponge?

Does Earth want another moon for a little more tidal romance?

Can land pick your birth place or would you like to live in the finest motherland?

Didn't the gerbil or turtle find any kind of hurtle to rhyme with purple?

Does time have another meaning without numbers?

Can you create a force that's irreversible?

How do you get your money back when there is no currency available?

Do fantasies vary in your surrounding reality?

Isn't there a lifetime membership which picks up the checks of destiny?

Is your career worth your weight in gold?

Are you so phony that you can't stop using a cell phone?

What if only one fruit was sort of the truth?

Can someone bribe you to go buy a clue?

Are there electro-magnetic theories polarizing you?

Are you happier with a digital dream more than a human one?

Is there anyone who understands a formula without an equal equation?

Ain't is kind of a word, but why ain't it used in a spelling bee?

Will you help re-size the shape of phony baloney?

Shouldn't one be reincarnated to remember a history?

Why can't you believe in a fairytale of nonfiction?

Are there accurate answers to fictional questions?

Who made fiction so worthy of listening?

Are you romanced by a southern or northern borealis?

Will you enlighten yourself with some high frequency
harmonics?

Who knows the meaning of an invisible word?

Can you live a day without the rest of the world?

Will you let someone transmit your thoughts for a day?

Are your findings getting lost everywhere you play?

Aren't there more math problems yet to be unsolved?

If time gets frozen, how much heat is needed for it to
thaw?

Why aren't we learning something old every new day?

Has anyone else seen a catfish walking over to another
lake?

Were there more zeros than ones when a program was
first made?

Do computers dot all their i's and cross all their t's better
than humans?
Would you disbelieve the truth if it was never written?
Is life about having fun or having more freedom?

Do movie stars dream about a movie never made before?
Why don't bubbles descend down from the top anymore?

Do ancient worlds have prehistoric issues merging in
with a new one?
Are you living for today, right now, this moment, or this
very second?

* * * * * * * * *

Does an outdated number trick about nine magicians at a
time?

Will they party harder like its 1999 when all new years
keep ending in 9s?

Where is the 9th wonder of the world you never hear
about?

Doesn't someone know about nine billion different ways
to make you smile?

Why can't you memorize nine different algorithms in
order to solve some cubes that are rubiks?

Sorry, have you been given the ninth degree on almost
everything?

Can you imagine someone sending you a homemade
afghan of loving 9s?

Will we ever celebrate a World Holiday considering
everyone works at least 9 hours, 9 days or 9 years?

Isn't 9 about the most creative time for all of mankind?

* * * * * * * * *

Are you warping in the next time zone to get ahead of yourself?

Don't organic songs graciously surround the beauty of earth?

Doesn't the population know about the majority of thoughts you've encountered?

Is there a secret recipe that can't ever be discovered?

Isn't there a heavenly hell boiling in an ice fire cube somewhere?

Shouldn't smokers start investing in air purifiers?

Is it possible to do anything anymore without any kind of interruption?

How many turns will make it right in order to go in the opposite direction?

Are you enduring the past, present, or future before your time comes?

Would you like to live in the ocean for a fishy horizon?

Will everyone know why who wrote what, when, and where?

Have you seen an ancient flame manifesting an eternal fire?

Do plants talk dirty when they have no water?

How many towns are pollinated with timeless flowers?

Does your spirit fight for your divine body?

Will you bid an enemy for a final quest of glory?

Doesn't electricity have a grounding effect with a shocking anecdote?

Do some books ever choose you to borrow a vote?

Aren't there some invisible laws someone should know about?

Can you get lost in a nightmare of paradise?

Do genies create their own mirage and vanish?

Have you figured out how to get a piece of the grand pie?

Have you solved a riddle without wondering why?

Aren't you better at your own monologue than anyone else in the world?

Is a writer worth more than just the richest words on record?

Why did so many Blues turn into a hockey team, color, or musical melodies?
Haven't professors proven a bogus theory is working accurately?

Are you paying for a ruling created over 99 or 999 years ago?
Can't you listen to almost anything you want, whenever you want to?

Have you followed all the rules and yet still flunking out?
Which side of the web would you like to crawl about?

Are you criminally mistreated because it's the law?
Can't a crazy person explain why things are more normally flawed?

Did you sneak out of the house to get away from the real world for a minute?

What poem could inspire a poet who didn't know it?

Can you hold true to your own word by the coincidence
of a coin?
What are the chances we can share a same dream?

Do friends just want you to be happy no matter how
much happiness can truly bring?
Is destiny riding along with eternity in perfect harmony?

How did a dictionary get its true meaning?
Does such a thing just explain itself?
Have you heard about any bots downloading themselves?

How many other red seas will be parted by another man?
Doesn't love mean exactly what you want it to mean?

Are any supernovas outgrowing their own universal
youth?
Isn't there a solution to every problem or just more
problems in this one solution?

Are you a hypnotizing fantasy or reality?

Can nature be foretold as a pleasure, fantasy, or prophesy?

Does one man or one nation offer a constitution of peace?

Doesn't honey have an age old secret made out of beeswax?

Is your family tree rooted back to the oldest sap?

Can you make a magic trick disappear as the final act?

Will parents always worry about more things they can't possibly imagine?

Isn't it possible Santa can mail everything over-night?

Is it impossible to sleep-in at a sleep-over?

Does one word have more meanings than any other?

Are there wars fought with bullets which don't have any holy meaning?

Will you always have to see to believe what's happening?

Do feelings wander in the opposite direction of your actions?

Whatever happened to taking as much time as you wanted?

When have you given war a piece of your mind?

If you found out losing could be fun, would you lose all the time?

Which court of the law holds a truth libel?

What kind of spell checker was used for the bible?

What were the first letters or words written on?

What sand stones were meant for original writing?

Do your desires melt away like chocolate on your tongue?

Have you ever burned out some circuits to get the job
done?

Isn't a fire a poor man's television?

Is there a degree in nothing anyone has graduated with?

Does everything become some kind of antique?

Is there a 0.0% chance of nothing ever happening?

Would a blind man recognize a designer's clothing?

Can you survive using your opposite hand for just a day?

If you could speak in any language, what's not to say?

Doesn't it feel cheaper to work out for free?

Are you engineered to think organically or mechanically?

Aren't we missing out already on futuristic paid holidays?

Have you been programmed to digest the same code
every day?
When there was only one language, did everyone know
almost everything?
Are you aware of the deep emotional sea waiting for the
country?

Is there a law for every rule or ruler?
How precious is the tiniest of all sea creatures?

Can a judge find you guilty of being so innocent?
Is there a composing grand theory for the greatest
musicians?

Are there some cold explanations for negatives with some
red hot answers to something positive?
Have you seen something lately you never knew existed?

Do borders justify lines on a map or where they happen
to be located?
How many boogers is the boogey man begetting without
being forgotten?

Are there hidden facts without any virtual meanings?

Do emotions evolve with some critical thinking?

Have you ever heard about a movie that wrote itself into
its own book?

How many re-takes will be made to record the greatest
track?

Are you willing to give up a favorite dream for a favorite
companion?

What violence persuades a final resolution?

Do Israelites find the historical peace within Israel?

Is it possible to meet your future life incognito?

Who can peace so many opposing pieces apart?

Isn't happiness found someplace in your heart?

Would one be thinking brighter if the universe was whiter?

Is death a matter of time or just a time that matters?

Does ancient ancestry follow us around forever?

How many pleasures does it take to get the center of the universe?

Does smoking enhance the flavor of dying?

Doesn't politics steal the agenda away from the party?

Where is the final destination of your creativity?

Weren't you the right writer writing with so many wrongly written words without any actual rightful copyrights?

A girl named Pearl with lots of curls came across a rural squirrel called Earl who liked to swirl, twirl, and whirl around the world by hurling a nut inside one lonely pearl.

And for the last time, we only inscribed a sign with a benign line of nine kinds designed with a fine divine wine of twines all behind the rhyming pleasure of number 9.

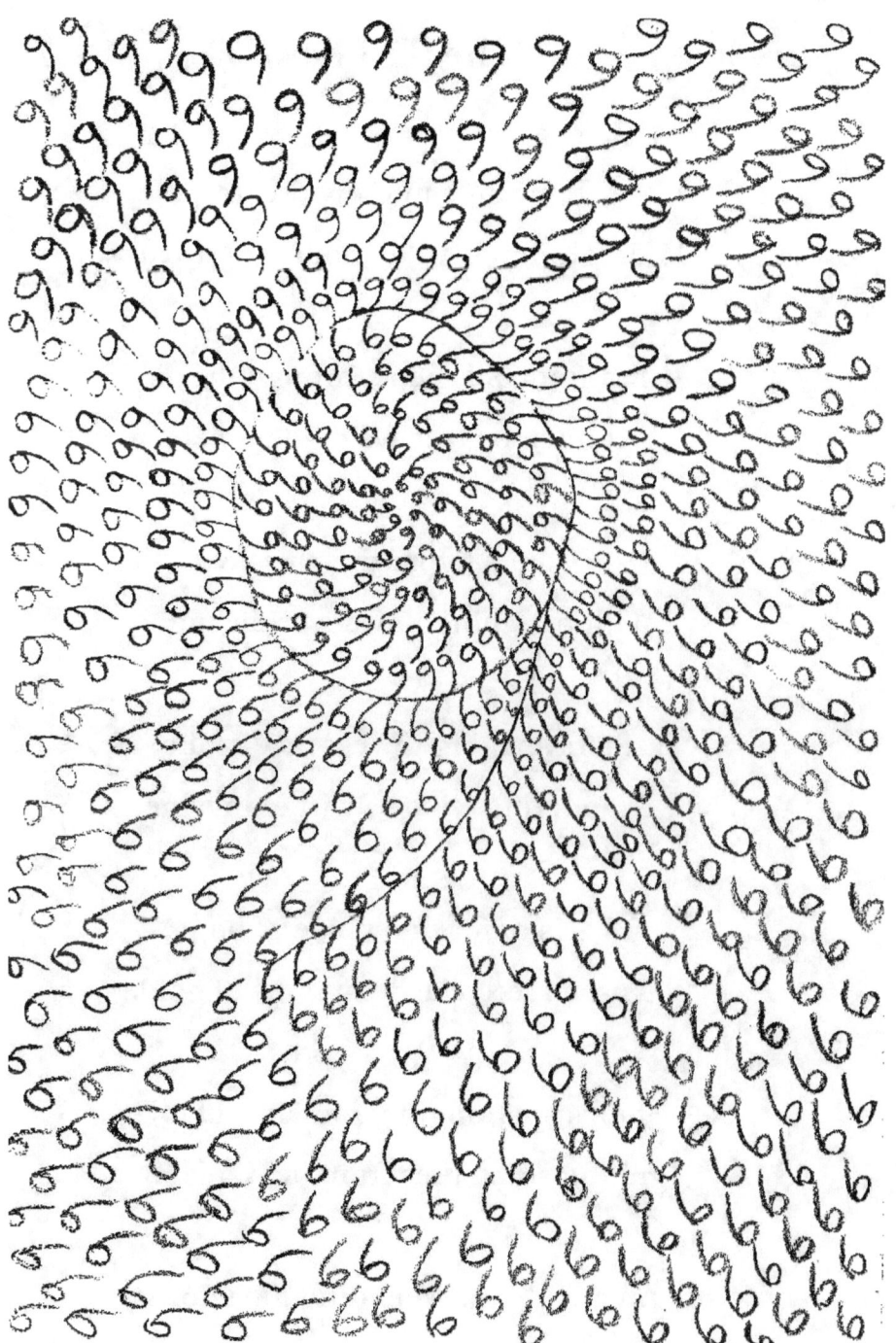

49

The 9th Poem

Time sifts into my dreams,
Midnight bugs wake mountain streams,

A bitter cold seeps through the air,
It must be true we made it here,

Colors hypnotize the sky,
With matching flowers of the night,

Stars shaping the essence of life,
Wandering willows wither in wine,

Tales of fortune made of hope,
Turned into clay with hints of gold,

Stones sparking the romance of love,
Igniting some fires from heaven above,

An angel kiss ascending nine doves,
Captured my spirit by surrounding a cove.

Special thanks to my loving family, friends, Arc Designs, Beethoven Elementary, Brockton Elementary, Community Magnet Elementary, Laurel Elementary, Roscomare Elementary, West Hollywood Elementary, and Westwood Charter Elementary for all your caring support throughout many great lasting years!

Thank you, Lord God!

Experience more 9th pleasures at

<u>www.the9thpleasure.com</u>

The 9th Pleasure

www.ingramcontent.com/pod-product-compliance
Lightning Source LLC
Chambersburg PA
CBHW050912120626
46552CB00004B/1544